D0461136

Surf Angel

Written by Terry & Heather Kraszewski

Illustrated by Bonnie Bright

Copyright © 2009 by Terry & Heather Kraszewski

All rights reserved. No part of this publication, either text or illustrations, may
be copied, reproduced, translated, printed or transmitted in any form or by any
means, electronic or mechanical, including printing, photocopying, electronically
copying or by any information storage and retrieval system, without the written
approval of the author, except for brief extracts by a reviewer for inclusion in
critical articles or reviews.

Published by: Surf Angel Publications   www.surfangelbook.com

ISBN:978-0-9821989-0-2   Library of Congress PCN: 2008910369   10 9 8 7 6 5 4 3 2 1

Printed in China

This Book Belongs to:

_____

Surf Angel is dedicated
to the angels in our lives who guide and inspire us,
and the lovers of the ocean who respect and
protect its beauty and wonder.

The Surf Angel dwells
In heavens above,
Waiting for sunset,
A time that she loves.

When children and seababies
Have finished their day,
Weary and tired
From a long day of play.

Surf Angel rides on her
Gossamer cloud,
Gliding to seashore
Where waves splash out loud.

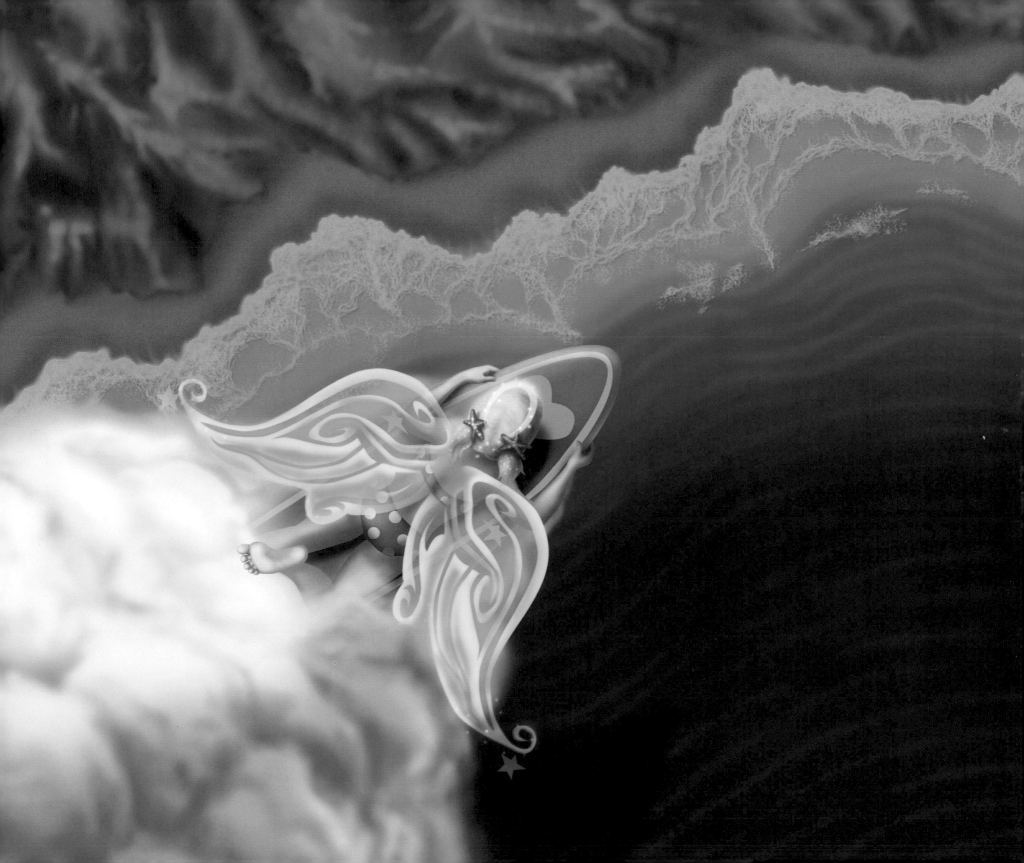

Time for bed,
The day is ending.
Moonrise is coming
And darkness is pending.

Huddle up and cuddle up
Where you need to be.
Nighttime is falling
On sand and the sea.

As sea fans sway
To and fro,
Surf Angel appears,
A starry glow.

She watches over the sea and the fish.
A safe night of sleep is her only wish.
Surveying the kingdom under the sea,
Until it's safe as safe can be.

The sea lions are a happy bunch,
Tummies full of squid from lunch.
They rode the surf, laid in the sun,
Sand is their bed when day is done.

Gentle giants form a pod.
Rocking slowly, the babies nod,
Against mom's body, snuggled close,
Baby whale rests, what he needs most.

Below the depths of azure blue,
Are baby dolphins, sweet and new.
Frolicking they do by day.
Nighttime comes, they sleep away.

Moonlight rays make quicksilver shimmers.
Mother sea turtle finds her swimmers.
Sparkles and phosphorus light up the night.
They're sound asleep, shells closed up tight.

Seahorse Dad rounds up his young.
"Giddy-up youngin's, the day is done.
Settle down now, no time to ponder.
Your beds are awaitin', over yonder."

Surf Angel checks on the starfish below,
Nestled on rocks, in moonlight they glow.
Bracing against the rising tide,
Awash in the twilight, safely they hide.

Cute and furry, fast and sleek,
The otters are tired and ready for sleep.
Tucked sweetly in their soft kelp beds,
Closing their eyes and resting their heads.

Fish swimming back and forth in their schools,
Are gathered together near the tide pools.
Crabs that side-walk across the wet sand,
Are picked up and tucked into crannies by hand.

Now we're all ready for a great night of sleep.
The creatures are resting without a peep.
Surf Angel lifts up her magical hand,
As stars sparkle down to the water and sand.

She gently begins a slow, sea fan sway.
"It's time to close up, it's the end of the day.
So, tuck into your shells and close your eyes.
Let your dreams take you up to the stars in the sky.

"Where I will be watching throughout the night,
Guarding my precious friends by moonlight."

Surf Your Dreams!

Terry Winn - Kraszewski

grew up in sunny Southern California, soaking up the sunshine, saltwater and a love of the surfing lifestyle.

Terry has a degree in Early Childhood Development. Living near the ocean has been a wonderful place to raise two beautiful and talented daughters.

Terry owns a surf boutique called *Ocean Girl* in La Jolla, California, which features her own brand of surf inspired clothing called *Surf Angel*.

An "anything is possible" attitude created her optimistic approach and involvement in issues ranging from protecting the environment to finding the cure for Cystic Fibrosis.

Heather Dawn Kraszewski

Heather was diagnosed with Cystic Fibrosis at four months of age. Living a positive life full of laughter, she inspires and teaches valuable lessons about how life should be enjoyed and treasured each and every day.

Heather has a degree in Film and Television and has worked on many television shows and feature films. She is also a gifted writer and story teller.

Having the beach as her playground, Heather has always felt a strong connection with the sea and the wonderful animals that share the ocean with her.

Bonnie Bright

Bonnie grew up in Malibu. Her parents, Mike Bright (surfing and beach volleyball legend and Olympian) and Patti Bright (volleyball Olympian and all around great mom) taught her a love for the beach and the value of hard work. When Bonnie is not busy producing artwork for clients, she enjoys her favorite pass times—playing beach volleyball, paddling and watching the sunset.

In addition to book illustration, Bonnie Bright's art and animation appear on a wide range of educational computer games. Her other creative talents include portraits, 3D background art, 2D animation and web design. Bonnie is a full time, freelance artist and enjoys a healthy balance between hard work, volleyball, and family.

Kathy Kohner Zuckerman
❄aka the real Gidget❄

has become the surfing icon for generations. Transcending time, Kathy has inspired the youthful optimism and spirit that still allows us to dream.

Kathy lectures around the country sharing her delightful stories about those wonderful days in Malibu, so long ago.

If you're lucky, you just might see the "Gidget" dropping in on a wave at Malibu, as she is still surfing and living her dream.

"This magical *Surf Angel* book combines so many things that I cherish. As a surfer who loves the healing ocean, and a father of three daughters, there is an automatic connection between *Surf Angel* and me. What an easy and wonderful way to share a special story and to make a difference."

~ Laird Hamilton
(Dad and big wave surfer)

~ Make A Difference ~
Contact Your Local Chapter

...adding tomorrows every day.

www.cff.org

www.surfrider.org